Pebble® Plus

Investigate the Seasons
Let's Look at Summer

by Sarah L. Schuette

Consulting Editor: Gail Saunders-Smith, PhD

Capstone press®

Mankato, Minnesota

Pebble Plus is published by Capstone Press,
151 Good Counsel Drive, P.O. Box 669, Mankato, Minnesota 56002.
www.capstonepub.com

Library of Congress Cataloging-in-Publication Data
Schuette, Sarah L., 1976–
    Let's look at summer / by Sarah L. Schuette.
    p. cm.—(Pebble plus. Investigate the seasons)
    Summary: "Simple text and photographs present what happens to the weather, animals, and
plants in summer"—Provided by publisher.
    Includes bibliographical references and index.
    ISBN-13: 978-0-7368-6708-5 (hardcover)
    ISBN-10: 0-7368-6708-2 (hardcover)
    1. Animal behavior—Juvenile literature. 2. Summer—Juvenile literature. I. Title. II. Series.
QL753.S383 2007
508.2—dc22   2006020452

Editorial Credits
Martha E. H. Rustad, editor; Bobbi J. Wyss, set designer; Veronica Bianchini, book designer; Kara Birr,
    photo researcher; Scott Thoms, photo editor

Photo Credits
Bruce Coleman Inc./Kim Taylor, 11
Corbis/Donna Disario, cover (background tree)
Getty Images Inc./Photographer's Choice/Darrell Gulin, 14–15; Photographer's Choice/Gail Shumway, 13;
    Photonica/Farhad J. Parsa, 7
Shutterstock/Andre Nantel, 20–21; bora ucak, cover, 1 (magnifying glass); Christopher, 1 (sun); Joe Gough,
cover (inset leaf); Kotelnikov Sergey, 18–19; Brian Erickson, 5
UNICORN Stock Photos/Jim Shippee, 16–17; Paula J. Harrington, 8–9

The author dedicates this book to her neighbor, Helen Reinhardt of Henderson, Minnesota.

Note to Parents and Teachers

The Investigate the Seasons set supports national science standards related to weather
and climate. This book describes and illustrates summer. The images support early
readers in understanding the text. The repetition of words and phrases helps early
readers learn new words. This book also introduces early readers to subject-specific
vocabulary words, which are defined in the Glossary section. Early readers may need
assistance to read some words and to use the Table of Contents, Glossary, Read More,
Internet Sites, and Index sections of the book.

Printed in the United States of America in North Mankato, Minnesota.
012011   006047R

Table of Contents

It's Summer!

How do you know

it's summer?

The temperature rises.

It's the warmest season.

The sun shines high
in the sky.
Summer days are
the longest of the year.

Animals in Summer

What do animals do
in summer?

Deer rest in the shade
to keep cool.

Tadpoles grow
into young frogs.
They find lots of bugs to eat.

Fireflies light up

on summer nights.

They flash to find mates.

Plants in Summer

What happens to plants
in summer?
Trees are full
of green leaves.

Plump cherries hang
from branches.
They are a tasty
summer treat.

Sunflowers turn

toward the sun.

They grow taller

with the warm sunshine.

What's Next?

The weather gets colder.

Summer is over.

What season comes next?

Glossary

mate—a partner or one of a pair; fireflies flash their lights to attract mates.

season—one of the four parts of the year; winter, spring, summer, and fall are seasons.

shade—an area out of the sun

tadpole—a young frog; tadpoles hatch from eggs and swim in water.

temperature—the measure of how hot or cold something is

Read More

Davis, Rebecca Fjelland. *Beaches and Bicycles: A Summer Counting Book.* Counting Books. Mankato, Minn.: Capstone Press, 2006.

Latta, Sara L. *What Happens in Summer?* I Like the Seasons! Berkeley Heights, N.J.: Enslow, 2006.

Rustad, Martha E. H. *Today Is Hot.* How's the Weather? Mankato, Minn.: Capstone Press, 2006.

Internet Sites

FactHound offers a safe, fun way to find Internet sites related to this book. All of the sites on FactHound have been researched by our staff.

Here's how:

1. Visit *www.facthound.com*

2. Choose your grade level.

3. Type in this book ID **0736867082** for age-appropriate sites. You may also browse subjects by clicking on letters, or by clicking on pictures and words.

4. Click on the **Fetch It** button.

FactHound will fetch the best sites for you!

Index

Word Count: 110
Grade: 1
Early-Intervention Level: 13